GULLIVER'S TRAVELS

GULLIVER'S TRAVELS

JONATHAN SWIFT

Retold by
Raymond James

Illustrated by
S.D. Schindler

Troll Associates

Library of Congress Cataloging-in-Publication Data

James, Raymond.
   Gulliver's travels / by Jonathan Swift; retold by Raymond James;
illustrated by S.D. Schindler.
     p.   cm.—(Troll illustrated classics)
   Summary: The voyages of an Englishman carry him to such strange
places as Lilliput, where people are six inches tall; Brobdingnag, a
land of giants; and a country ruled by horses.
   ISBN 0-8167-1865-2 (lib. bdg.)   ISBN 0-8167-1866-0 (pbk.)
   [1. Fantasy.] I. Schindler, S.D., ill. II. Swift, Jonathan,
1667-1745. Gulliver's travels. III. Title.
PZ7.J1543Gu 1990
[Fic]—dc20   89-33943

Printed in the United States of America.
10 9 8 7 6 5 4 3 2 1

Huge waves pounded against the sides of the *Antelope*. Wind and rain lashed everyone on deck. Six months ago, we had left Bristol, England, to do some trading in the East Indies. But the storm we had been fighting the past few days had grown worse, blowing the ship far off course. Twelve crew members had already died. The rest were very weak. As ship's surgeon, I did the best I could for them.

"Gulliver! Lemuel Gulliver!" shouted the captain to me. "Let down the longboat now!"

"Aye, Captain," I shouted back at him. Carefully, five crew members and I lowered the longboat. But no sooner were we in it than the ship smashed against an immense rock. The *Antelope* split apart, sinking rapidly. The captain and crew members still on board went down with her.

Only the six of us made it clear of the ship. We rowed until our backs and arms ached. Then, without warning, a tremendous wave crashed down on us, knocking all of us overboard. I saw a few hands reaching up from under the water. A moment later, they slipped beneath the waves forever.

I swam with all my might. I had no idea where I was going. Soon, I let the wind and tide take me along. I was too tired to resist.

When I felt I couldn't swim another stroke, my foot scraped against bottom. Land! I thought. I swam forward with what little strength I had left. After a while, I could stand on both feet, and I could see the dim outline of an island. I was standing on a long, wide slope of sand that extended from the shoreline.

I walked nearly a mile before I finally reached the beach. It was getting dark now. The moon looked like a wafer I could reach out and eat. My stomach growled at the thought, and fatigue overwhelmed me. When I came to a patch of soft grass, I decided to rest there for the night.

I awoke the next day to discover I couldn't move. My arms and legs were tied with strings and pegged to the ground. My hair, which was long and thick, had also been tied down. I was flat on my back, helpless.

Suddenly, I felt something moving on my left leg. A wild animal? I wondered. I held my breath. The creature advanced forward over my chest and came up almost to my chin. I blinked hard, not believing what I saw. It was a man less than six inches tall! He held a tiny bow and arrow in his hands. And I could feel at least another forty of these pint-sized creatures creeping up behind him on my body.

I cried out in surprise. All of the little creatures jumped back in fear, some leaping off my sides to the ground. I struggled to get free. After a few tugs, I managed to pull out the pegs holding my left arm to the ground. I also pulled up my hair to the point where I could turn my head slightly.

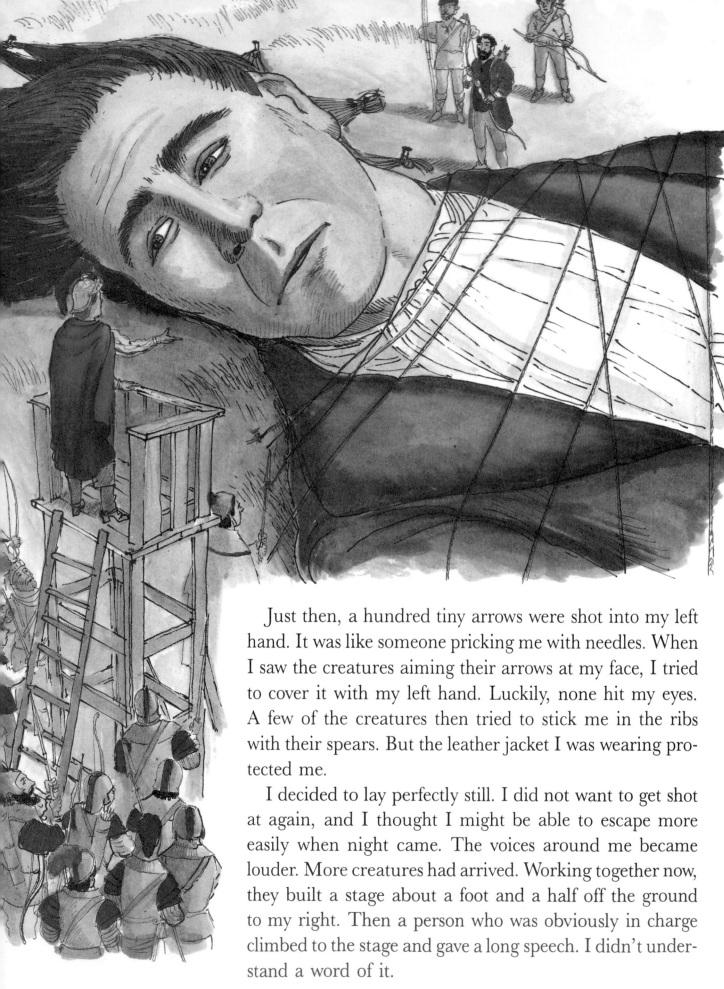

Just then, a hundred tiny arrows were shot into my left hand. It was like someone pricking me with needles. When I saw the creatures aiming their arrows at my face, I tried to cover it with my left hand. Luckily, none hit my eyes. A few of the creatures then tried to stick me in the ribs with their spears. But the leather jacket I was wearing protected me.

I decided to lay perfectly still. I did not want to get shot at again, and I thought I might be able to escape more easily when night came. The voices around me became louder. More creatures had arrived. Working together now, they built a stage about a foot and a half off the ground to my right. Then a person who was obviously in charge climbed to the stage and gave a long speech. I didn't understand a word of it.

After the speaker finished, fifty of the little creatures came over and cut the strings binding the left side of my head. I could now turn my head to the right. Starved, I pointed a finger at my mouth, hoping the speaker would understand. He nodded, then commanded that several ladders be placed against my sides. Over a hundred tiny men climbed the ladders, carrying baskets filled with meat and bread on their shoulders. I gulped down the food three baskets at a time. They stared at me in awe. They had never seen such an appetite before!

After eating, I indicated I wanted a drink. The creatures used ropes and pulleys to hoist two barrels no bigger than small mugs to my chest. Then they rolled the barrels close to my mouth. A sweet wine flowed out, and I drank the barrels dry in seconds.

Once I finished my meal, a person who looked of higher rank than the speaker before climbed up to my collarbone. He spoke to me for about ten minutes, and I understood him no better than the other speaker. Then a group of the creatures rubbed my skin with ointment. It soothed the areas where the arrows had struck. I was also given more wine, and I drank as much as they were willing to offer me. But then, I felt dizzy. The sky above me started to spin. And just before I passed out, I realized a sleeping potion had been mixed into the wine I drank.

A sudden jolt to my back woke me up. Opening my eyes, I saw the leaves of trees moving past me overhead. I was being transported, but how? I turned my head as far as it would go. From what I could see and from the rumbling noise underneath me, I knew I was riding on top of a wooden cart. It was at least seven feet long and four feet wide, and I guessed it was about three inches high. In front of my head were nearly two thousand horses pulling the cart. None was bigger than my middle finger.

Occasionally, we stopped along the way. One of those times, three curious natives crept near my face. They poked their spears up my nostrils. To them, my nose must have looked like a pair of cave openings. But one of the spears tickled my left nostril. *Ah-choo!* I sneezed. All three natives flew backward. They were more startled than hurt. But none ever came close to my nose again.

At last, we arrived in front of the gates to a city. The emperor of this kingdom, which I learned was called Lilliput, came out with his court to meet us. His name was longer than he was: Golbasto Momaren Evlame Gurdilo Shefin Mully Ully Gue. He spoke briefly, then pointed to an ancient temple not far from the city. I was taken and chained there. My left leg was bound with a chain made of ninety-one of their largest chains. Then they locked this one big chain with thirty-six padlocks. The Lilliputians looped this chain, which was about two yards long, through one of the lower windows of the temple and secured it.

Chained as I was, I could still stand up and walk around a little. Beyond the walls of the temple, I could see the countryside. The tallest trees were only seven feet high. Open fields looked like small gardens. Lakes looked like puddles. Hills looked like grassy bumps. What a strange land!

And what a strange creature *I* must have seemed to the thousands of Lilliputians who came to gaze at me. They all wanted to see *Quinbus Flestrin*. That's what they called me. Later, I found out it meant the Great Man Mountain.

In the days and weeks that followed, the Lilliputians and I became more used to each other. They made a bed for me that was actually six hundred of their own beds sewed together. They also made me blankets and sheets. To help feed me, the emperor commanded that all the villages within nine hundred yards of the city deliver six cattle, forty sheep, and an equal amount of bread and wine every day. He also assigned six hundred people to act as my servants. Over three hundred tailors were ordered to make me clothes like those worn by the Lilliputians themselves. And six court scholars were given the task of teaching me the spoken language of Lilliput. I learned this native tongue quickly.

These favors, however, were granted on one condition: that I allow two of His Majesty's men to search my original clothing. I agreed. With pen, ink, and paper, they jotted down what they found: a comb, a watch, some coins, a razor for shaving, a pistol, a knife, a horn of gunpowder, and lead shot. To the men, of course, the comb looked like a fence, the knife like a saber, and the coins like silver platters. They had no clue what the pistol was used for. The same was true for the gunpowder, razor, and lead shot.

What they didn't find were my eyeglasses and a small spyglass. These were hidden in a private pocket inside my jacket. I wanted to keep my glasses to protect my eyes from any more arrows. And I knew the spyglass would come in handy if any ship passed by the island. Rescue by sea was always on my mind.

As time wore on, I became eager for my freedom. Again and again, I humbly asked His Majesty to unchain me. Finally, he said yes, although one of his cabinet members, Skyresh Bolgolam, was against me. But first, I had to agree to their demands. I was not to leave Lilliput without permission. I had to watch where I walked so I wouldn't accidentally trample the Lilliputians or their homes. And I had to help the Lilliputians against their enemy, the Blefuscudians, on the island of Blefuscu about eight hundred yards away across the channel. I cheerfully said yes to all these demands, and my chain was unlocked. For the first time since I set foot on Lilliput, I was free!

Two weeks after I gained my freedom, I was visited by His Majesty's Secretary of Private Affairs, Reldresal. He told me that a Blefuscu fleet of fifty warships was soon going to set sail and invade Lilliput.

I was determined to help the Lilliputians defeat their foe. I made fifty sturdy cables by twisting together three of the Lilliputians' strongest, longest cables for each one I needed. To the ends of these fifty cables, I attached iron hooks. I intended to tie up each of the fifty Blefuscu warships and drag them all to Lilliput.

I walked to the northeast side of Lilliput, which was just across the channel from Blefuscu. Keeping hidden from view, I removed my shoes and some of my clothing but left my jacket on. Then, grasping the cables and hooks, I slipped into the water and waded toward Blefuscu. It took me no more than half an hour to reach the fleet. And because the channel was no deeper than six feet in spots, I could practically walk on the bottom.

At the sight of me coming near them, the Blefuscu sailors dove overboard in terror and swam to shore. There, about thirty thousand Blefuscudians gathered together. I ignored them, taking my cables and hooks and linking each ship with the others. It was then that Blefuscu archers shot their arrows at me. They stuck in my hands, neck, and face. I was especially worried about some hitting my eyes. I put on my eyeglasses. They shielded my eyes from the thousands of arrows now raining down on me.

Without delay, I took out my knife and slit the anchor lines holding the ships. Then, taking the cable ends in my hand, I started back toward Lilliput. Behind me I could hear the shouts and screams of the Blefuscudians as they watched me haul off the pride of their navy. Halfway across the channel, I stopped to remove my glasses and the arrows still stuck in my skin. Then I moved on, with fifty ships trailing behind me. I was now in full sight of Lilliput's northeastern beach.

The emperor and his entire cabinet were waiting for me there. I held up the cable ends and shouted, "Long live the most powerful emperor of Lilliput!" Loud cheers greeted me from His Majesty and everyone with him. I anchored the Blefuscu fleet just off the shoreline, tying the cable ends around a rock in the water. And when I walked ashore, the emperor strode up to me and made me a *Nardac*. This was Lilliput's highest honor, and I was proud to receive it.

The moment of my greatest triumph was also the beginning of my troubles. The emperor insisted that I return to Blefuscu and capture the rest of the navy. He wanted to seize control of the island and make it part of his own kingdom and enslave all the people there.

I told him bluntly that my conscience would never allow me to bring such a brave and free people as the Blefuscudians into slavery. Slavery was wrong. The deep frown on His Majesty's face showed how unhappy he was with my refusal.

Three weeks later, an ambassador and some high-ranking officials from Blefuscu arrived at Lilliput to sign a peace treaty. The signing went quickly, and the terms of the treaty weighed heavily in Lilliput's favor. Then, on behalf of Blefuscu's emperor, the ambassador invited me to visit the island. This time, however, it would be a friendly visit. I asked Lilliput's emperor for permission to go. He gave it to me grudgingly. I was to leave in a few days.

But before that time came, I was paid a late-night visit by a person from His Majesty's court who had taken a liking to me. He told me that my enemy at the court, Skyresh Bolgolam, now had an ally in Flimnap, the Lord High Treasurer. Flimnap hated to see Lilliput's treasury being drained in order to keep me fed, clothed, and housed.

Together, Skyresh Bolgolam and Flimnap advised the emperor to bring charges of treason and other crimes against me. And His Majesty, who never forgave my refusal to conquer the Blefuscudians, eventually agreed.

I couldn't believe my ears. I asked what the emperor planned to do to me. My visitor said that at first, death was recommended. The temple where I slept would be torched, and I would be shot full of poisonous arrows as I slept. Another suggestion was that my shirt be doused with poisonous juice. This would make me tear my own flesh. I would die in torture—and by my own hand.

Secretary of Private Affairs Reldresal pleaded for my life, said my visitor. It was then that His Majesty decreed blindness as my punishment. Twenty of the emperor's surgeons would shoot arrows directly at my eyes.

My visitor now grew silent. I could tell something else was bothering him. I asked him what it was. He then said that I was to be *told* my punishment would be blindness only. However, the emperor and his advisers, especially Bolgolam and Flimnap, also agreed in private to starve me to death. All of this would occur three days from now.

My thoughts raced inside my head. What should I do? I knew I couldn't stay in Lilliput. In three days, I would be blind and on my way to being starved. I had to get away. But where? The only place I could think of was Blefuscu. After all, I *had* been invited there. I'd just arrive a couple of days early.

Before sunlight the next morning, I gathered up my personal belongings and quietly set out for Blefuscu. I borrowed one of Lilliput's own ships and stowed my gear in it. Then, pulling the ship behind me, I swam across the channel. How odd it felt to be going for help to a country I helped defeat!

The sun was rising in the eastern sky by the time I came ashore. Word of my arrival spread rapidly. Soon I was met by two guides sent by Blefuscu's emperor. They directed me to the capital city. There, the emperor came out to greet me. He was surprised to see me so soon.

During the next three days, both the emperor and his subjects treated me very well. They gave me a comfortable place to sleep and plenty of food and drink. Feeling safe and content, I wandered down by Blefuscu's coastline. I walked along the edge of the sea, until something caught my eye about a hundred yards out in the water. Curious, I removed my shoes and stockings and swam out near the object. It was a small boat floating upside down! It must have overturned during a recent storm. I dove underneath the boat and examined it closely. For the most part, the boat was undamaged. All I needed was to get it ashore.

With the help of Blefuscu's remaining fleet, I did just that. As soon as the boat touched sand, I flipped it over and hauled it up on the beach to work on it. The materials I needed for repairs were provided by Blefuscu craftsmen. It took ten days of hard, steady work before it was finished. I put the boat in the water. Her sail billowed in the breeze, and she floated without so much as a single leak.

19

The emperor of Blefuscu was happy to see me leave. He felt Lilliput and Blefuscu would both be better off without such a giant as myself to take care of. He gave me as much food and drink as I would likely need for the journey, plus live cattle and sheep. I thanked him for his generosity. Then, waving farewell to him and his people, I sailed out to sea. Finally, after nearly two years on these two islands, I was once more on open waters.

Soon I was picked up by an English vessel sailing homeward from Japan. I was taken on board and promptly told the captain my story. He scratched his head in disbelief. Then I pulled out of my pocket the live cattle and sheep given to me by Blefuscu's emperor. The captain's eyes sparkled in amazement. I told him I'd give him a cow and a sheep when we docked in England.

We pulled into port at Downs on April 13, 1702. The voyage went pleasantly enough, although a rat had carried away one of the sheep I had. I found its bones picked clean in a hole near the galley. The surviving sheep and cattle I brought home with me to Redriff.

There, my wife and two children ran out to greet me. We hugged and kissed each other tenderly. It had been a very long time since we'd seen each other. We held each other's hands and entered the house.

Inside, my young son and daughter laughed when I told them about the Lilliputians and Blefuscudians. They were still laughing as I reached into my pocket. When I pulled out my hand and opened it, both children gasped. For there, standing on my palm, was *living* proof.

Only two months passed before I became restless again. I sold the cattle and sheep I had brought back with me from Blefuscu. I gave the money to my wife, kissed her and the children goodbye, and headed off for my next sea voyage. On June 20, 1702, I left on the *Adventure*, a well-named ship, I thought.

Bad luck dogged the ship soon after we rounded the Cape of Good Hope. A southern monsoon, one of the most dangerous storms a seaman could sail into, took us by surprise. Our sails were torn in two, and the storm blew us many miles off course. When it finally died down, we cast off a longboat and rowed toward an island. We hoped to take on fresh water.

As the other crew members went about their jobs along the beach, I decided to explore inland. I must have walked a mile or so before I tired and turned back. But when I got to the beach again, I saw the crew members rowing furiously in the longboat. It was already halfway toward the anchored ship. I was just about to call out after them to return for me when I saw a huge creature bounding into the sea after them. Luckily, the longboat had a good head start, or the giant would have overtaken it.

As fast as I could, I ran inland. Before I knew it, I was running through a field where the grass was twenty feet high. Cornstalks rose forty feet in the air. Close by was a hedge at least one hundred twenty feet tall. And there were trees whose tops I could not see.

I was out of breath and leaning on a blade of grass when my heart leaped into my throat. Only fifty yards away and coming straight toward me was a man as large as the one that chased the longboat. He was taller than a church steeple. Each step he took was at least ten yards long.

I dashed into a clump of fallen corn, shaking with fear. Then the man called out. Seven more giants arrived. They held in their hands long, curved blades. Back and forth they swung them along the ground, cutting huge amounts of grass. All eight of them were moving closer and closer to where I was hiding. Would I be cut in half like a blade of grass? Would I be squashed like a beetle underneath their feet? Would one of them pick me up and pop me in his mouth like a bread crumb?

Whoosh! A cutting blade came within a few inches of me, and I screamed. The man in the lead stopped swinging his blade and crouched down toward me. He moved aside the corn covering me and lifted me up with his index finger and thumb. I was now sixty feet off the ground, and he brought me within three yards of his eyes. I didn't squirm. Instead, I folded my hands in prayer and softly asked that he spare my life.

The giant seemed pleased with the sound of my voice. And he was surprised that I could speak, though he obviously didn't understand me. He put me in the breast pocket of his coat and rushed off to a man who must have been his master.

The farmer who owned the field gaped at me when the worker pulled me from his pocket. He called together all the field workers and asked if any had seen another creature like me. They all shook their heads. Then the farmer spoke to me. His voice boomed in my ears, nearly deafening me. I didn't understand anything he said. But it didn't seem to matter to him. He scooped me up, placed me in his handkerchief, and slipped it and me into his coat pocket.

When the farmer showed me to his wife, she let out a bloodcurdling scream. It was as if she had just seen a toad or a spider. But after a while, seeing how gentle and soft-spoken I was, she grew very fond of me. She sat me down at the kitchen table and served dinner to me, her husband, her mother, and two of her three children.

What a meal it was, too! On a plate twenty-four feet in diameter was a mound of cooked meat and potatoes. The farmer's wife minced a bit of meat for me and also crumbled some bread. She then gave me a thimble of cider.

During the meal, the woman's cat leaped up on her lap. The animal was three times the size of an ox. Then the farmer's four dogs trudged in. Each was as large as four elephants combined. And finally a nurse came in with a one-year-old boy in her arms. He was the youngest of the farmer's children.

As soon as the baby saw me, he cried. His hands reached out for me. To him, I was a new toy. The farmer's wife picked me up and held me out toward the boy.

Suddenly, the baby grabbed me by the waist and stuck me in his mouth. I roared so loudly that the infant dropped me in fright. If the child's mother had not caught me in her apron, I would have surely broken my neck. Still crying, the baby was given a rattle to play with. It was an enormous wooden drum with boulders inside, and it was attached to a long, thick wooden pole.

Dinner had made me sleepy. When the farmer's wife saw me yawning, she picked me up and took me to her bedroom. She put me on top of her bed and covered me with a clean, white handkerchief. It was as big as a ship's sail and a foot thick. The bed itself was twenty yards wide and eight yards off the floor. And the bedroom was three hundred feet square and over two hundred feet high. I slept soundly, dreaming of my wife and two children back home.

Something stirring on the bed woke me. Opening my eyes, I saw two bloodshot, saucer-sized eyes peering at me a yard away. It was a gigantic rat! I grabbed my sword just before this gruesome animal sprang at me. It fell right on my sword point. I pushed the dead rodent off me and measured it from snout to tail. It was over six feet long!

When the farmer's wife finally entered the bedroom, she shrieked at the sight of the blood on the bed. I stood up and smiled to show her that I was unharmed. Relieved, she picked up the dead rat with a pair of tongs and tossed it out the window.

I was taught the language of this strange race of giants by the farmer's daughter. Nine years old, she was considered small for her age—just forty feet tall. But she was very kind toward me. After learning the language of the Brobdingnagians—that was what the people of Brobdingnag were called—I named the farmer's daughter *Glumdalclitch*. It means "little nurse." She, in turn, called me *Grildrig*. It means "little man." We became dear friends.

The girl's father, though, proved far less kind. He saw me as a way of making some easy money. He put me in a small box with some tiny holes punched in the top for air and a tiny door cut into one of the sides. Then he mounted his horse, strapping me to his saddle. Glumdalclitch followed behind on a horse of her own.

Finally, he got off his horse and started posting some signs in the marketplace. They announced to one and all that a strange, tiny creature resembling a human being and able to speak several words and perform several tricks would be on display inside the inn.

Soon the inn was crowded with townspeople. They were all eager to see the strange creature and willing to pay for the privilege. The farmer collected their coins while Glumdalclitch sat beside the table I was placed on. Then the girl told me to walk around the table, which I did. She asked me questions and I answered them in Brobdingnagian. She poured some drink into a thimble. I took it in both hands and drank it down. I even took out my sword and flashed it in front of me. I did all of this for no fewer than twelve separate groups of onlookers. They just stood by the table, blinking and pinching themselves to be sure this wasn't a dream.

The next day, I repeated the whole show. I performed for eight hours without a rest. By the end of the day, I could barely whisper. I was exhausted.

Still, the farmer was not satisfied. For the next ten weeks, I was shown in eighteen large towns as well as in many villages and family homes. Glumdalclitch tended to me as best as she could. The girl could see how tired and worn-out I was. Yet she could not persuade her father to slow down. We must have traveled thousands of miles by the time we arrived in the capital city of Lorbrulgrud. There, ten times a day, I was shown to the wonder and amazement of all those citizens who paid the farmer's price to see me.

Soon, the queen of Brobdingnag summoned the farmer, Glumdalclitch, and me to the palace. When the queen held out her little finger to me, I clutched it in both my hands and kissed it respectfully. Her Majesty was delighted.

Right there, she asked the farmer if he would sell me to her. Seeing how frail I was, the farmer said yes. The price he wanted was a thousand pieces of gold. Her Majesty didn't hesitate. She clapped her hands. Within seconds, a servant came in carrying a sack bulging with gold coins. The farmer greedily took it from him and slung it over his shoulder.

Now that I was the property of the queen, I humbly asked her if Glumdalclitch could stay with me. Glumdalclitch nodded her head, and so did Her Majesty. And the farmer gave his consent, too. He was glad that his daughter would live among royalty and be out of his care.

Everyone in the palace, the king included, was happy to have me there. Everyone, that is, except the queen's favorite dwarf. Before I came, he was the smallest man in the kingdom—just under thirty feet tall. Now, he was the second smallest and no longer special. The dwarf hated me.

During the first meal I ate with Her Majesty, the dwarf suddenly seized me and dropped me into a bowl of cream. Luckily, Glumdalclitch saw what happened and fished me out. But I must have swallowed over a quart of cream.

Another time, when I was in the palace gardens, the dwarf shook some apple trees hanging over my head. Apples as big and heavy as barrels crashed down around me. One of them grazed my head, knocking me flat to the ground. Still, I was not hurt. The dwarf was spared a whipping at my request. The queen, however, sent him away from the palace.

Even with the dwarf gone, I continued to have problems because of my size. Once, a small spaniel lapped me up in its mouth and carried me in its teeth to its master. I was nothing more than a mouse to be toyed with and shown like a trophy to the dog's owner.

Another time, a frog jumped into a trough where I was sailing a small boat made for me by the queen's carpenter. The frog leaped into the boat, and it was all I could do to keep it balanced on the water. Finally, as the boat was about to turn over, I took an oar and bopped the frog on the nose. It croaked loudly and slid overboard, leaving me in peace.

There was one animal, however, that was not so easily avoided. That was the monkey owned by one of the cooks in the kitchen. One day, when no one was near, the monkey snatched me and took off through an open window. The monkey, holding me in one of its paws, scooted along the rain gutters of the palace. Soon it was up on the roof. A chambermaid shaking out a rug from a bedroom window saw the monkey with me struggling in its grasp. She yelled for help.

Down below, Glumdalclitch came running with a number of servants behind her. She shrieked when she saw me in the monkey's paw over three hundred yards above the palace grounds. Ladders were now placed against the walls. When the monkey saw all this, it dropped me on the ledge and fled.

The wind blew around me, and I clung as tightly as I could to the ledge. Then I started to slide off. I would have plunged to certain death if one of the servants on the ladders had not grabbed me in the nick of time. He put me into his shirt pocket and brought me safely down.

Glumdalclitch now refused to leave my sight. Both she and the queen were concerned about my safety. Her Majesty commanded that a special wooden traveling box be made for me. It was strongly built and watertight. The only openings were two windows on the sides and a square hole cut into the top of the box. I could open and shut this square hole with a board that slid back and forth in a groove. There was also a small ring on top of the box for carrying it.

Inside, I slung a hammock from the four corners at the top. That way, I wouldn't be so violently jostled during journeys by horse. The inside was also quilted to prevent injury from a fall. I found this home away from the palace quite comfortable.

Glumdalclitch and I would take small trips together. She would ride on horseback, while I lay in my hammock inside the box she fastened to the rear of her saddle.

A journey we took to the southern coast of Brobding-nag, however, resulted in Glumdalclitch getting very ill. I was eager to see the ocean again, however, and I begged Glumdalclitch to let me go there. From her sickbed, she reluctantly agreed. But she insisted that a servant accompany me.

The servant took me to the seashore in my special traveling box. He placed it on the sand beyond the reach of the surf. As he moved off to hunt for birds' eggs among the rocks, I opened a window and breathed in the fresh air. I watched the waves tumble against the beach, and their steady motion made me drowsy. I closed the window, hopped up into my hammock, and napped peacefully.

I have no idea how long I slept. All I know is that I awoke with a start. There was a strong yank on the ring of my traveling box. Suddenly, I could feel the box lift off the sand, rise high in the air, then hurtle forward at tremendous speed. What was happening?

I got down from my hammock and shouted out. But there was no reply. I opened a window. To my astonishment, I saw nothing but clouds and blue sky. Then, I heard a loud flapping overhead. Peeking further out of the window, I saw the head of an eagle. The eagle was holding my box in its claws. The eagle probably thought I was some kind of turtle and the box was my shell. And that meant it would fly until it could shatter the box on a rock and eat its contents—me!

As I tried to think of a way to save myself, I heard the flutter of many more wings outside. The box was banged and I was knocked from side to side. It could only mean that other eagles were now trying to steal the box for themselves. A beak darted briefly inside my open window. I shut it immediately, plunging myself into darkness. I climbed back into my hammock and tucked my knees under my chin, shivering with fear.

Then, it happened. The eagle, unable to fend off the other birds, dropped the box. The next thing I heard and felt was a tremendous splash. But the box I was in continued to descend. After a while, I could feel it rise slowly, then pop to the surface. Only a trickle of seawater seeped in. Both windows were below the waterline, and I could not slide open the hole on top of the box. I was trapped!

Hours passed. There was no food, no water, and, I thought, no hope. My little traveling home would become my coffin.

I was lost in misery when something scraped against the side of the box. I held my breath. I could hear the sound of voices and ropes and pulleys being placed around the box. Suddenly, the box was rising out of the water. A voice boomed, ''If anyone is below, speak!'' I pleaded from a window to be released from this floating prison.

When the overhead board was sawed through, a ladder dropped, and a man my size climbed down it. I was once more among people my own height and strength! The sailor helped me up on board the ship. I was taken directly to the captain's cabin, where I told my story about Brobding-nag. The captain must have thought I was stark raving mad. But soon he believed me—if only because of the extraordinary detail with which I told my story.

We sailed on and on. At last, the ship came into port. I thanked the captain and crew for saving my life and set out for my home. As I walked up the front path to my house, my wife raced outside and embraced me. My daughter and son also came out and hugged me. It had been four years since I'd last seen them, but now we were all together again.

The craving for travel, for new adventures, took me away from home again. Waving farewell to my family, I started off to Portsmouth, where my next voyage—this time as captain—would begin.

The ship headed out to sea. We sailed toward the South Sea Islands, where we hoped to trade. The weather was fair, and the ocean was calm. All was going well.

Then, tragedy struck. Disease swept through the ship, killing many of my crew. I had no choice but to sail to Barbados and recruit new crew members. The men I hired were a hardhearted lot.

Just *how* hardhearted they were became clear to me a few days later. I was sitting in my cabin, going over some sea charts, when a gang of them burst through my door and tied me up. With rum and talk of treasure, the new recruits convinced the original crew to join the mutiny. I was now a prisoner in my own cabin and at their mercy.

I remained tied up in my cabin for weeks. At last, several crew members came for me. They cut the ropes binding my feet, but they left my hands tied behind my back. Grabbing my arms, they led me up on deck and put me in a longboat. They rowed the longboat out to a strip of sand just off an island. They pushed me out of the longboat and tossed a small bundle and my sword after me. Then they rowed back to the ship.

Fumbling with the sword, I managed to cut the ropes that bound my hands behind me. I slung the sword from my waist, picked up the bundle, and walked toward the beach. I looked up and down the beach, but saw no living creature. It was then that I decided to move inland.

Before long, I came upon fields of oats and grass, where I saw several animals. What strange creatures they were! They had heads and chests covered with thick hair, beards like goats, and brown skin. They had no tails, moved on all fours, and had long claws. They could spring and run with great skill. Yet I must confess that in all my travels, I had never seen animals more disgusting than the ones I was watching now. They were filthy and foul smelling.

Suddenly, one of them rushed headlong toward me. I swatted the creature with the blunt end of my sword. The animal howled in pain, attracting some forty more toward me. As quickly as I could, I climbed up a nearby tree. But the beasts were nimbler than I imagined. A few climbed the tree after me, and it was a struggle to keep them at bay with my sword.

Suddenly, they all scurried away. Shading my eyes with my hand, I looked out over the field. There, in the distance, a horse walked quietly. He was the only animal in view. Why one horse would frighten away a whole pack of these beasts, I couldn't say. I slid down the tree, and the horse picked up my scent and galloped over to block my way. He seemed shocked at the sight of me. The horse neighed a few times. A second horse came up beside him now. The two stared at me. Then the pair moved off a little as if to discuss what to do with me. I had never seen such behavior before in animals.

Two words I overheard them saying were *Yahoo* and *Houyhnhnm*. Both horses were looking at me when they spoke the first word. I had no idea what the second word meant. And because *Yahoo* was easier to say than *Houyhnhnm*, I said *Yahoo* in a loud voice to be friendly. The horses nodded their heads and gestured for me to follow them.

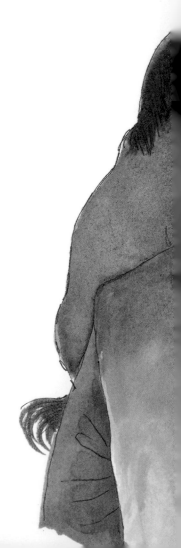

They led me to a wooden building. The roof was low and covered with straw. One of the horses ushered me into the building. When I got inside, I couldn't believe my eyes. There were five horses sitting down—some were eating, others were doing simple chores. If I didn't know they were horses, I'd have sworn they were a family—a *human* family.

The two horses that led me to this building nudged me out through the back door and into an open area. There was another building behind the house we had just left. When I entered this building, the stench nearly brought me to my knees. Inside were three of those ugly, filthy creatures I had first met. They were feeding upon roots and the flesh of mules and dogs. One of the horses said *Yahoo* several times, indicating the beasts. Then the same horse looked at me and said *Yahoo*.

I was thunderstruck. These horses considered *me* a Yahoo. But the closer I looked at the beasts, the more I realized how similar they were in size and shape to me. The front feet of the Yahoos differed from my hands only in the length of their fingernails, their rough palms, and their hairy skin. They also walked on all fours, while I walked on my two feet only. Apart from that—and some sorely needed soap and water—the Yahoos might easily have passed for human. What land *was* this, I wondered, where horses ruled humans or, at least, humanlike creatures? And what would become of me, a Yahoo?

The horses, who I finally learned were called Houyhnhnms, knew I was not like other Yahoos. They treated me decently and built a small home for me between their own house and the place where they kept the Yahoos. Soon, I learned their language. The word *Houyhnhnm* in their language meant "the perfection of nature." The word *Yahoo* meant the opposite. And when I told the Houyhnhnms of my own land, a place where humans ruled over horses, they were clearly shocked. In fact, they still had not recovered from the first shock of a Yahoo able to speak.

One of the horses asked me how I came to their country. I told him about the great ship I captained and about the mutiny. The horses looked surprised. One of them said he understood how Yahoos could rebel against authority. That happened all the time. But he was still puzzled how the Yahoos of my country ever learned to build a ship. Dumb, filthy brutes such as the Yahoos were good only for the simplest of tasks, they told me.

I tried to explain, but from their eyes I could tell they didn't believe me. And to be honest, I couldn't blame them. These horses were intelligent, well-groomed, and just. The Yahoos were anything but.

The months passed swiftly. During my stay among the Houyhnhnms, I grew to respect and, yes, love them. They were governed by reason and by nature. Friendship and kindness were the two main virtues they lived by. Evil and fighting were practically unknown among them and were always linked to the Yahoos.

When I told the Houyhnhnms about the wars my own country had had with other lands, they didn't understand what I was talking about. I explained to them that war was waged by my country when it wanted things another country had or when another country wanted things my country had. Then the two countries fought until they took our things or we took theirs.

The Houyhnhnms pointed to my hands, feet, and face. How could creatures with short, flat-edged teeth, soft, clawless hands, and a slow, awkward walk on just two hind legs ever hope to fight well? I answered that the Yahoos in my country and other countries had weapons for such a purpose.

I was lucky that the Houyhnhnms regarded me as different from other Yahoos. But that difference also troubled them. Some of the horses were afraid that I might mingle with my own kind and perhaps lead the Yahoos against them. I told them I had no desire even to be seen, let alone mingle, with the beasts. Still other horses thought it wasn't right for a Yahoo to be treated almost like a Houyhnhnm. More and more, the feeling that I didn't belong as a Houyhnhnm *or* a Yahoo increased among the horses.

My master, a proud horse who showed me great kindness and patience, took me aside one morning. He told me that a number of prominent Houyhnhnms had gotten together recently to decide my fate. Their decision was for me to leave their island in three months.

I was staggered by this news. For three years I had been living among them. I had hoped to live out my life on the island. Now, I would be forced back to my own country and among my own kind—Yahoos.

But the decision was final, and sadly I did as I was told. I built a crude kind of canoe in six weeks. Then I made two paddles from oak branches. I tried out the finished canoe in a small pond. It floated, and I hoped it would hold up until I could reach another shore in it.

The day came when I had to say farewell to my adopted Houyhnhnm family and friends. Tears filled my eyes as I stepped into the canoe and waved at the horses gathered along the beach. I was already out to sea when I heard one of the Houyhnhnms cry out, *"Hnuy illa nyha, majah Yahoo!"* It meant ''Take care of yourself, gentle Yahoo!''

I paddled the canoe for hour after hour. The sun beat down upon my back. The wind was against me. The muscles in my arms stiffened as I paddled onward—to where, I didn't know. Finally, I saw the shoreline of an island and headed toward it. That night I slept on the beach.

The next morning, I was awakened by the yells of savages running toward me. I jumped up and pulled the canoe back into the water. Furiously, I paddled out to sea again. The natives shot their arrows at me. I was lucky to escape with my life.

But as I paddled farther away from the island, I caught sight of a sail on the horizon. I decided I'd rather risk the savages on the beach than the Yahoos on the ship. I paddled even faster now. No natives were on the beach. Luck was still with me, I thought. I hid my canoe among some shoreline trees and myself among some bushes nearby.

A small boat full of sailors was soon launched from the ship. The boat beached close to where I and my canoe were hidden. It wasn't long before one of the sailors found me lying face down under some ferns.

The sailors took me in their small boat to the ship anchored offshore. There, I told the captain about my life among the Houyhnhnms. He didn't believe a word I told him. But he agreed to take me as far as his own ship was going, Lisbon. From there, he said, I could catch another ship back to England.

In December 1715, I finally reached England. Soon, I was knocking on the front door of my house. My wife and children greeted me with great surprise and joy. Then, I stepped inside the house.

I was home.

Date Due
